MY THOUGHTS ARE CLOUDS

Poems for

MINDFULNESS

Georgia Heard

illustrated by **Isabel Roxas**

Roaring Brook Press

New York

Also by Georgia Heard

Falling Down the Page

The Arrow Finds Its Mark

Published by Roaring Brook Press

Roaring Brook Press is a division of Holtzbrinck Publishing Holdings Limited Partnership

120 Broadway, New York, NY 10271 • mackids.com

Library of Congress Control Number: 2020912222

ISBN 978-1-250-24468-0

Our books may be purchased in bulk for promotional, educational, or business use. Please contact your local bookseller or the Macmillan Corporate and Premium Sales Department at (800) 221-7945 ext. 5442 or by email at MacmillanSpecialMarkets@macmillan.com.

First edition, 2021 • Book design by Aram Kim

Printed in China by Toppan Leefung Ltd., Dongguan City, Guangdong Province

1   3   5   7   9   10   8   6   4   2

my gratitude to

Dermot Obrien   Leo Obrien

Rebecca Kai Dotlich   Patti & Bill McNaught

Elizabeth Harding   Kate Jacobs

Megan Abbate   Isabel Roxas

Avia Perez   Aram Kim

GM & MN

CONTENTS

MINDFUL WORLD

MEDITATION

KINDFULNESS

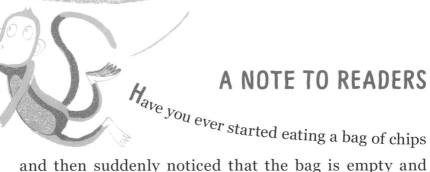

A NOTE TO READERS

Have you ever started eating a bag of chips and then suddenly noticed that the bag is empty and you've eaten all of them? Or have you ever been walking somewhere and arrived at your destination, only to realize that you remember nothing about how you got there? Or sat in class and heard the bell ring and not recalled anything that went on during the period? It probably means you've been on autopilot: You were busy thinking about other things and not fully present in your life. I call it having "monkey mind." Monkey mind is when your mind jumps around like a monkey swinging from thought-tree to thought-tree, distracting you from whatever you're doing in the present moment.

Mindfulness is the opposite. It's when you're focused on the present. You're not thinking about the past or anticipating the future. You're aware of where you are, what you're doing, and what you're thinking and feeling in the moment.

Being present is more difficult than it sounds. Sometimes the mind is quiet and you can pay attention to what's happening *now*. But sometimes it isn't. Most of us are mindful some of the time in little slices and pieces of our day. For example, you might be fully present when you watch the first snowflakes swirling outside your window, or when you lean in to listen to your friend telling you a secret, or when you bite into a piece of delicious chocolate and savor its creamy taste. No one is perfectly mindful every single minute of the day, but all of us can become more and more present and aware.

Just like shooting free throws or playing the piano, the more you practice mindfulness, the easier it becomes. Mindfulness tools can help you steer your mind back to the present without negative judgment when it wanders. It's not about numbing uncomfortable feelings and forcing yourself not to have any thoughts. Instead, mindfulness teaches you to be aware of your thoughts and experience your feelings as they come without being overwhelmed by them.

I hope that reading these poems will inspire you to practice mindfulness, teach you to get in touch not only with your own feelings but also with the feelings of others, allow you to feel calmer, more joyful, more focused, less anxious, and to find the space and peace to live in the present moment.

Inside My Mind

ihavesomanythoughtsinmyheadandicantstopthem
fromracinglikeafasttrainwhathomeworkwillihave
whatgradewilligetamismartenoughwhatsthatnoiseim
afraidwhowillsitwithmeatlunchidonthaveanyfriends
inthisclassimsadbecausemygrandmaissickimissmy
dadimnotsurewhattodomyteacherisfunnyineed
anewpairofshoessometimesidontlikethewayilook
imboredihopeididntforgettobringmynotebookhow
canistopthisrunawaytraininsidemymind...

Quiz: How Mindful Are You?

Answer *yes* or *no*. There are no right or wrong answers.

Are you always in a hurry?
Is your mind full of worry?

Does your pulse beat fast?
Do you dwell on the past?

Do you feel jumpy when you have to wait?
Are you absentminded and usually late?

Do you feel uneasy deep inside?
Are your feelings on a roller-coaster ride?

If you answered YES
to these questions—
don't distress!

Being mindful is the answer,
and here's the first step how—
bring yourself back
to the HERE AND NOW.

There Is a Monkey in My Mind

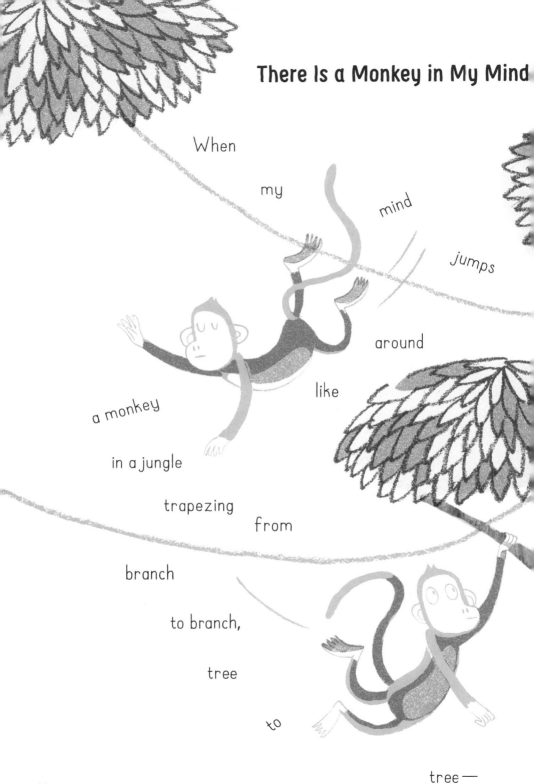

When

my

mind

jumps

around

like

a monkey

in a jungle

trapezing

from

branch

to branch,

tree

to

tree—

10

I tell myself:

Be kind

to

the monkey

swinging

in

my

mind,

and give it

space—

then lead it

gently to

a peaceful

place.

11

BREATHE IN BREATHE OUT

Focusing on your breath is a type of mindful practice where you use the inhale and exhale of your breath to anchor your mind. Take a few deep breaths and follow each one in and out. When you notice your thoughts wandering, or you feel anxious or overwhelmed, redirect your attention back to your breath and try to release your thoughts. You can practice mindful breathing anytime.

Take deep breaths. Feel less stress.

Riddle

what do you do

20 times per minute,

30,000 times per day,

10 million times per year,

without trying,

without thinking,

without knowing?

(turn the page for the answer)

BREATHE

take a deep breath

Counting Breaths

inhale	+	exhale	**ONE**
inhale	+	exhale	**TWO**
inhale	+	exhale	THREE
inhale	+	exhale	FOUR
inhale	+	exhale	FIVE

Breathe   in and out

                                until counting

F A D E S   INTO   BREATH

inhale	+	exhale	SIX
inhale	+	exhale	SEVEN
inhale	+	exhale	EIGHT
inhale	+	exhale	
inhale	+	exhale	

Ocean Breath

Ride the wave

of your breath.

In-breath...

Out-breath...

Your breath

rolls in,

your breath

streams

out;

it ebbs

and

flows

like the rhythm of a rising and falling tide.

Ride the wave

of your breath

and find the calm within.

Square Breathing

is a type of breath work you can use to calm yourself down when faced with stress or when you're feeling overwhelmed.

How to Do Square Breathing:

- Find a comfortable place to sit.
- Breathe in through your nose for a count of 4.
- Hold your breath for a count of 4.
- Breathe out through your mouth for a count of 4.
- At the bottom of your breath, pause and hold for a count of 4.
- Repeat four times.

Your Breath Has Its Own Language

In Sanskrit, breath is *prana*.

In Hebrew: *ruach*.

In Greek: *pneuma*.

Trees breathe.

Animals breathe.

Oceans breathe.

Planet Earth breathes.

Your breath

has its own language,

and if you listen

closely

you will

become fluent

in its smooth syllables:

swift or slow = *worried or calm*

short or long = *tense or relaxed*

shallow or deep = *sad or happy*

Your breath

is the translator

of your

heart.

In and Out Breath

Breathe in.

Breathe out.

Breathe in kind.

Breathe out unkind.

Breathe in quiet.

Breathe out noise.

Breathe in hope.

Breathe out fear.

Breathe in joy.

Breathe out worry.

Breathe in love.

Breathe out hate.

When My Noisy Mind Quiets

Here in this chair

my noisy mind

settles into quiet.

        I leave all my *to-do's*

        in a place

        asleep like winter trees.

Then I become friends

with the seasons of my breath,

and my own voice blossoms.

MINDFUL ME

*Mindfulness helps you get in touch with
your feelings and gives you the tools
for more self-acceptance.*

The

opposite

of

mindFULness

is

mindLESSness.

Selfie Moment

S L O W   D O W N

GET READY

HOLD YOUR MIND STEADY

CLICK

CAPTURE THE PRESENT MOMENT

LIKE A PICTURE IN YOUR MIND

Is My Space Bar

Of all the keys on my keyboard

the space bar is the one

I use the most.

Without the space bar

lettersandwordsjumbletogether.

When   I   touch   the   space

bar   inside,

I   unjumble   my   thoughts

and   put   my   mind

on   pause.

My Thoughts Are Clouds

I watch

my thoughts

sail by

like sweeps of clouds

dissolving

in a calming

sky.

I can't fall asleep

I'm feeling sad

I don't want to get a bad grade

I'm stressed out today

I miss my friends

I got in trouble at school

I'm anxious about homework

My Inner Weather Report

Yesterday

a fierce storm

blew in

with bolts of lightning

and thunderclaps.

Pitch-black clouds

hovered overhead,

and it poured

all day long.

Today

I feel

sunny

with gentle breezes

and no clouds at all.

I'm learning

to take my inner weather report—

and notice my feelings

as they come and go.

Be Here Now

tomorrow

future

later

plan on

should do

could do

will do

BE
HERE
NOW

yesterday

past

the other day

gone by

should have

could have

would have

Mindfulness Is Like a Mirror Haiku

(to read this poem, hold the page up to a mirror)

When I am mindful

I look into the mirror

at the inner me.

MINDFUL WORLD

Being mindful and becoming more aware of the present moment means noticing the sights, smells, sounds, touches, and tastes that you experience in the world around you.

When I become calm on the inside,

the world becomes calm on the outside.

Consider a Raisin

Consider a raisin.

Look at it like you've never seen it before.

Pinch it in your fingers.

Smell the raisin.

Place it in your mouth,

bite down—

what does it taste like?

(Maybe hundreds

of sunrises and sunsets

bursting sweet in your mouth,

or something else?)

Now consider

an apple,

a piece of chocolate,

even a french fry . . .

one

mindful

morsel

at

a

time.

Open Your Eyes

Turn off the television.

Put down your phone.

Notice one small, everyday thing

and gaze at it softly:

tiny salt crystals spilled on a kitchen table,

the fresh page of a new notebook

opened on your desk.

Lose yourself.

See like an ant

or a tree.

Focus your heart like a camera

and the ordinary will shine brand-new.

Nature Walk

Walk gently into a forest.

Kiss the ground with your feet.

Run your fingers over weathered bark.

Listen to tongues of leaves talking.

Gaze at sunlight resting in branches.

Smell sweet fresh air

breathed out by trees.

Let a forest's healing canopy

bathe you in peace.

In Japan, they practice something called *shinrin-yoku* (森林浴). *Shinrin* in Japanese means "forest" and *yoku* means "bath." So *shinrin-yoku* means bathing in the forest atmosphere, or taking in the forest through your senses. Forest baths help ease stress and worry and can help you relax.

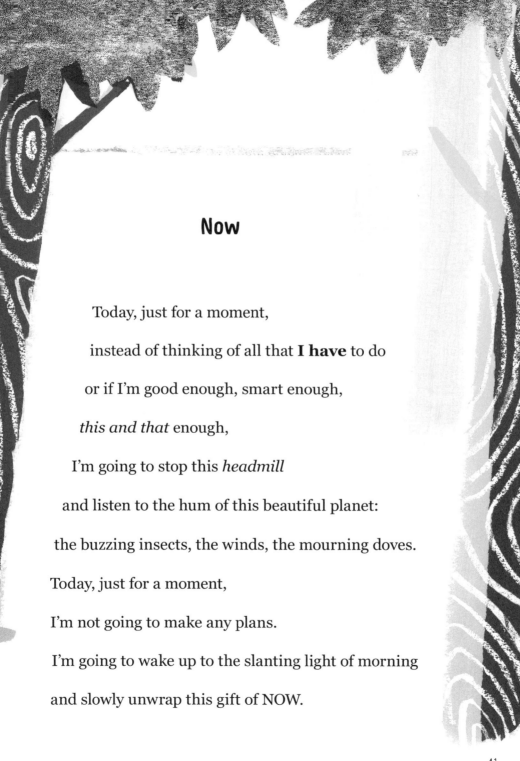

Now

Today, just for a moment,

instead of thinking of all that **I have** to do

or if I'm good enough, smart enough,

this and that enough,

I'm going to stop this *headmill*

and listen to the hum of this beautiful planet:

the buzzing insects, the winds, the mourning doves.

Today, just for a moment,

I'm not going to make any plans.

I'm going to wake up to the slanting light of morning

and slowly unwrap this gift of NOW.

MEDITATION

Meditation is not about sitting cross-legged for hours on a snowy mountaintop. Meditation is simply when you freeze-frame a small portion of time and try to be fully present. There are many different tools of meditation, from learning how to relax your body to repeating words to focus your mind.

Meditation is like

a snow globe:

all those shaken-up thoughts

drift

down

slowly

until your mind is clear.

Come Home to Your True Self

Find a quiet place to sit;
imagine your thoughts as clouds floating away

until your mind is a peaceful pond
where smooth waters mirror still sky.

See yourself walking in an open field;
let wind offer you its breath.

Become a green leaf
floating lazily down a stream.

Be vast like an ocean horizon
stretching yourself beyond what your eyes can see.

Now come back.
Come home to your true self.

Butterfly Body Scan

• Imagine: Your mind is a garden of flowers, and the warm sun touching your petals calms your thoughts. A peaceful butterfly flies in the sky and then comes to rest on top of your head.

• Follow the imaginary butterfly as it guides you in mentally "scanning" your body, to help bring awareness to parts that are tense.

Butterfly's tiny feet dance lightly on your scalp— opening your mind.

Take a few deep breaths and allow your face and throat to relax.

Butterfly's soft wings brush your face like a summer breeze— grazing over your eyelids, gliding over your cheeks and jaw, fluttering over your neck.

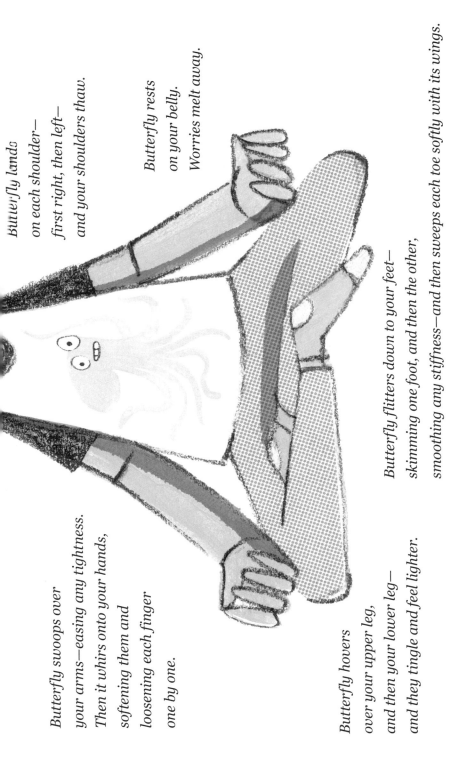

*Butterfly lands
on each shoulder—
first right, then left—
and your shoulders thaw.*

*Butterfly rests
on your belly.
Worries melt away.*

*Butterfly swoops over
your arms—easing any tightness.
Then it whirs onto your hands,
softening them and
loosening each finger
one by one.*

*Butterfly hovers
over your upper leg,
and then your lower leg—
and they tingle and feel lighter.*

*Butterfly flitters down to your feet—
skimming one foot, and then the other,
smoothing any stiffness—and then sweeps each toe softly with its wings.*

Take a few deep breaths and send a gentle smile of thanks to your imaginary butterfly as it floats back up to the sky.

Meditation Is Like Peeling an Onion

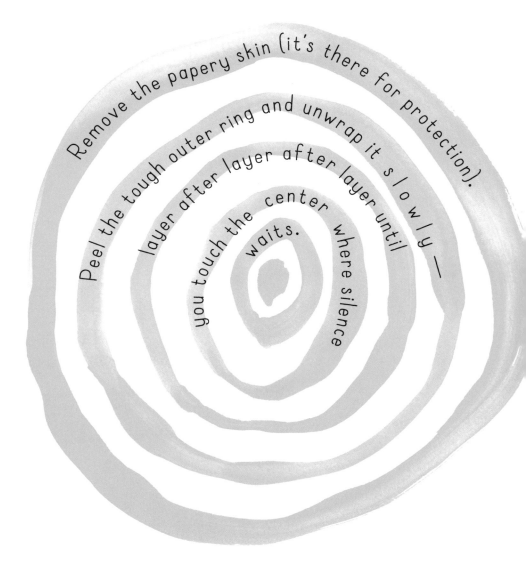

Remove the papery skin (it's there for protection). Peel the tough outer ring and unwrap it s l o w l y — layer after layer after layer until you touch the center where silence waits.

The Music of the Moment

Listen to the sounds around you

as they rise and pass away.

Let them touch your inner ear.

Slip inside each sound

and allow it to dissolve into air:

rain strumming on your roof, a dog barking far-off

in the night, a ceiling fan whispering . . .

When you sit in this room of quiet,

where listening ends

and thoughts end,

open yourself

to the music

inside you.

Empowerment Mantra* Haiku

I AM THE CHANGE

I AM GRATEFUL

LET IT GO

I AM PRESENT

DON'T LET YESTERDAY TAKE UP TOO MUCH OF TODAY

I AM ENOUGH

I SPEAK UP

Change the way you feel:

Choose a sticky-note mantra,

Post it on your heart.

Mantra comes from the Sanskrit word meaning "mind tool." It's a word or sound repeated during meditation to help you focus. Mantras are often words that bring comfort, positivity, and hopefulness, and you can repeat them throughout the day to calm your mind.

After Meditation

There is something brand-new about my world,

like when rain washes away gray skies

and makes my day brighter.

Then, I am like an artist:

repainting streets, buildings, trees

with bold, jazzy colors—

wild watermelon,

sunglow,

razzle-dazzle rose—

There is something brand-new about my world.

KINDFULNESS

Kindfulness is a mindful practice where you learn to open your heart and become more empathetic—to yourself, other people, and the world—and with this open heart you will learn ways to speak up for yourself and for justice and equality in the world around you.

Kindfulness Haiku

No act of kindness,

no matter how small or slight,

is ever wasted.

Cultivate Tenderness

In a world of sharp edges,

take a moment

to replay memories

that make you smile:

holding Grandpa's strong hand,

snuggling in your soft, much-loved blanket,

your mother's gentle good-night kiss on your forehead.

In a world of sharp edges,

take a moment

to remember

the tender things

in your life.

Three-Way Loving Kindness Meditation

Whisper these words to yourself:

May I be at peace.

May I be safe.

May I be filled with loving kindness.

Whisper these words toward

a friend or someone else:

May **you** be at peace.

May **you** be safe.

May **you** be filled with loving

kindness.

Whisper these words toward

the earth:

May **the earth** be at peace.

May **the earth** be safe.

May we fill **the earth** and all

creatures on it with loving

kindness.

Kindfulness

In English class,

we read a poem

by a poet whose name flows like a song:

Christina Rossetti.

HURT NO LIVING THING

Hurt no living thing:
Ladybird, nor butterfly,
Nor moth with dusty wing,
Nor cricket chirping cheerily,
Nor grasshopper so light of leap,
Nor dancing gnat, nor beetle fat,
Nor harmless worms that creep.

Our teacher told us

that being *mindful*

also means being *kindful*—

caring and speaking up

about the hurts in the world.

For homework, we wrote

our own poems like Christina Rossetti.

Here's mine:

HURT NO LIVING THING

indness should be what you bring
everyone you meet. Be kind to those who cry,
like the girl from a different country
sitting sad and alone at her desk about to weep.
Like your friend who's having a rough day.
Like the shy kid at recess too timid to play.
Be mindful in thought, in the words you speak.
Open your heart to the world; open it deep.

Your Heart Is Like a Flower

A flower doesn't need

to count how many raindrops it sips,

add up the number of bees tickling its petals,

tally the blooms that curl up and fade away.

Just as it is with you—

your heart doesn't need to keep track

of all its loves and losses;

it just needs to keep opening

and opening

and opening.